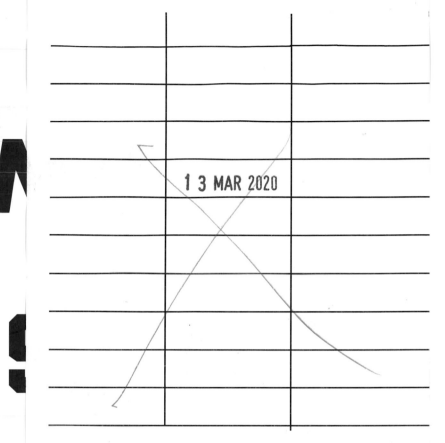

Original concept by
**Roger Hargreaves**

Written and illustrated by
**Adam Hargreaves**

Mr Wrong had just got a job as a tour guide at the Space Centre.

He was very proud of his new job, so he invited all his friends to the Space Centre to show them round.

Mr Wrong showed his friends the first spacecraft that had landed on the moon.

"This is the first kettle to land on the moon," explained Mr Wrong.

"That's not a kettle," said Little Miss Wise.

He showed them round the huge hall where the Saturn V rocket was kept.

And he showed them how to put on a space suit.

"I don't think that's quite right," said Little Miss Wise.

And then Mr Wrong took them outside where there were two rockets standing side by side.

"We can have a look inside Rocket Two," said Mr Wrong and they all travelled up in a lift to the hatch at the top of the rocket.

"Rocket One is going to be launched on a mission to Mars today," explained Mr Wrong, pointing to the other rocket.

They climbed through the hatch and were all standing admiring the space capsule when, suddenly, there was a rumble.

A rumble that built into a roar.

A roar that made the rocket vibrate and shake.

The noise was extraordinary.

It was like a thousand elephants all trumpeting and stampeding at the same time.

Rocket Two had lifted off. They were on the wrong rocket. They were going into space!

Mr Wrong looked at all his friends and all his friends stared at Mr Wrong.

"Oops," he said, sheepishly.

The rocket soared into the sky leaving a great trail of smoke.

Mr Wrong and his friends stood in a huddle wondering what was going to happen next and then a hatch door opened.

It was an astronaut.

An astronaut who looked just as surprised as the rest of them.

"Who are you?" he exclaimed.

"We … we got on the wrong rocket," explained Little Miss Wise. "Who are you?"

"I am Captain Strongarm and we are on a mission to Mars!"

"Mars!" gulped Mr Worry. "Could you just take me home first?"

"I'm sorry, we can't return until we have completed our mission," said Captain Strongarm.

"Oops," said a small voice in the corner for the second time that day.

"Can you show us where we are going?" asked Little Miss Wise.

"Sure, this is our solar system and there are eight planets. This is Earth and this is Mars," the Captain said, pointing to a large screen. "This is the sun. We don't want to get too close to that because the sun is so hot. We would sizzle like a sausage!"

"Sausages," murmured Mr Greedy. "Yummy."

There were lots of strange things in space.

For one, there was no gravity and they all found themselves floating about the cabin.

Mr Topsy-Turvy did not know whether he was the right way up or the wrong side down.

But then Mr Topsy-Turvy is very used to that feeling.

They found a black
hole and Captain
Strongarm explained
to them that there was
nothing in a black hole.

Even so, Mr Nosey, being the
nosy fellow he was, had to go
outside and have a look!

On the way to Mars they had to carry out some repairs, which meant leaving the rocket to go out for a space walk.

Mr Lazy discovered that this was just the kind of walk that he liked.

Not so much walking, but more floating on his back.

Finally, after months flying through space they arrived on Mars.

To everyone's surprise they were not the first ones there.

"Is … is that a Martian?" asked Mr Worry, nervously, when they saw a tent.

Nobody had an answer. Not even Little Miss Wise.

But it wasn't a Martian, it was Mr Impossible.

On a camping trip.

"I always come here for the summer," said Mr Impossible.
"I like to get away from it all."

"That's impossible," said Captain Strongarm,
shaking his head in disbelief.

They unloaded the moon buggy, although Little Miss Wise did point out that it ought to be called the Mars buggy.

They had landed on a vast, flat plain of red dust.

There was nothing to see for miles around.

Except for one rock.

One rock that Mr Clumsy managed to drive into!

Suddenly, an alarm sounded.

"What's that?" shrieked Mr Worry, leaping into the air. Or, at least, he tried to leap into the air, but found that he was already there.

The alarm had rung because there was a meteor shower heading their way.

"Don't worry!" cried Mr Strong, who leapt into action.

He bounced around the surface catching the meteors and throwing them back into space.

After a few days on Mars it was time to go home.
Captain Strongarm started the rockets and they began to
rise into the air.

"Goodness gracious!" exclaimed Little Miss Wise. "We've left
Mr Small behind!"

"I can't stop the rocket now!" cried Captain Strongarm.

Poor Mr Small! He was so small nobody had noticed that he
was still on the surface.

He was going to be left behind
on Mars.

There was nothing
they could do!

Or so they all thought, until Mr Bounce jumped out of the rocket's hatch, grabbed Mr Small by the scruff of his space suit and bounced right back up to the safety of the rocket.

"That's what I call a bouncy ride!" cried Captain Strongarm.

Captain Strongarm was very pleased with the mission. It had been a great success and they had collected lots of samples to take back to Earth.

Mr Wrong looked at all the samples.

"It seems a very long way to come just to collect some rocks," he said. "There are lots of rocks back on Earth!"

On the way home they stopped at the International Space Station for tea.

"Where are the trains?" asked Mr Wrong.

"It's not that sort of station," sighed Little Miss Wise.

Mr Wrong also couldn't understand why their tea was not in a cup and saucer.

So Little Miss Wise showed him why.

While everyone else was having tea, Little Miss Naughty sneaked out and went for a ride on a satellite.

All the way around the Earth!

It only took ninety minutes for her to orbit the Earth and she was back in time to catch the space shuttle home.

The space shuttle plunged back through Earth's atmosphere with the same force that everyone had experienced when they had taken off.

They splashed down safely in the sea.

"Well," said Little Miss Wise to Mr Wrong, "I think I can safely say, that that was the very best tour any tour guide has ever taken me on!"

A very, very, very long way away, 140,000,000 miles to be as precise as Little Miss Wise, Mr Impossible settled down in his deck chair to enjoy some peace and quiet when a small voice said, "Hello."

It was a Martian.

That's impossible, I hear you say.

But is it?